Hood N*gga Season

By: Author Chan J

Printed in China

First Edition: 2025

ISBN: 9798316922512 (Paperback)

Written by Author Chan J

Published by TaylorsLegacyLLC

Dedication

I dedicate this
To my dedication.
To my motivation.
To my patience.
And to God's timing.

I dedicate this
To scratching things off the "to do list."
To my first time.
To my introduction.
And to getting my feet wet.

I dedicate this
To more to come.
To better with time.
And I hope you enjoy.

Wynter's Story

1

As my alarm clock went off on my phone, I rolled my eyes; I didn't feel like getting out of bed. I rolled over and closed my eyes, hoping for a few more minutes of sleep. I sucked my teeth; if I didn't get up, I knew I would miss work, and I knew damn well I wasn't missing no money. I was taking a break from school to focus on my money. After about 5 minutes, I got out of bed and stretched my arms to the ceiling.

"Damn, this job kicking my ass, but I need the hours," I groaned to myself. I walked into my bathroom and turned on the shower. I didn't care what time I was scheduled, and I was getting up at the last minute.

"Alexa, play Summer Walker," I said before showering. As Summer's sweet voice filled the bathroom, I quickly took a 15-minute shower and hopped out to wash my face. After taking care of my hygiene, I dried off and dropped my towel in front of the mirror. I admired my natural beauty as I fingered through my curly hair.

"Damn girl," I said, smiling. There wasn't a soul on this earth who could tell me I wasn't beautiful. Standing at 5'6, with full B-cup breasts, a flat stomach, a plump ass, and smooth chocolate skin, I was a dream. My full lips formed into a frown when I glanced at the clock on the nightstand.

“Now see, I always do this. Brittany is not about to get on my ass today. I’m not in the mood,” I said, rushing to my closet. Brittany was my manager and a bitch too. I worked at a shoe store in the mall. Although I was only 20, I needed a break after high school. I decided to get a job instead of going to college immediately.

School was a lot on me mentally, and with my kind of parents, it only added to the pressure. Nancy and Robert Lewis were the world’s greatest and toughest parents. My mom was a private school teacher, and my dad was a firefighter. We were what some people considered middle class, but that didn’t stop my parents from spoiling me. As I said, they were the greatest, but when I decided to work instead of college, they gave me hell. Especially my mom, she wasn’t going for that shit. They backed off when they quickly realized I would do what I wanted. Shit really hit the fan when I told them I was moving into my own apartment. I wanted my freedom and independence; I was tired of all the rules my parents set. I wasn't disrespectful by far, so I got the hell on.

I threw on my work shirt and some jeans along with my Jordans. I grabbed my phone, car keys, book bag, and purse and jetted for the door. It took me about 20 minutes to get to work, and I prayed traffic was on my side. I arrived at work with 5 minutes to make it to the store.

I rushed past the food court and looked down at my phone while running. I looked up and ran right into a man and fell on my ass.

"You okay?" he asked, holding out his hand.

"Yeah, I'm sorry, I'm just in a rush," I said, taking his hand.

"Slow down, baby. Next time, you may hurt yourself," he said.

"Yeah, thanks. My bad again," I said, taking off running. I didn't even pay attention to his ass. I was officially late for work. I ran past Sephora and rounded the corner into the shoe store.

"You're late again," Brittany said as soon as I ran in.

“My bad, I had trouble this morning,”

“No one likes excuses, Wynter. Either be on time or find another job,” she said.

“Alright,” I said, walking to the back

“And Wynter?”

“Yeah,”

“Restock the whole floor before customers arrive, and when you are done, take register two,” she said, smirking. I nodded and turned around, heading to the back.

“This bitch gets on my nerves,” I said.

“Bitchney, pissed you off too?” Randell, my gay co-worker, asked.

“Man, I was 2 minutes fucking late. My ass was running and ran right into someone,”

“Was he fine bitch?”

“Randell, I don’t know. I was just trying to make it here,” I said, laughing.

“Anytime I run into a nigga Ima see if he's fine or not,” he said, cracking his gum.

“Randell, anytime you run into a nigga you've probably been with him,” I said, laughing.

“True, true,” he said.

I put my stuff in my locker and grabbed shoes to stock the floor. The store was due to open in 1 hour, so I had to hurry up.

“I’m about to help you. There's no way you are stocking the whole store in an hour,” Randell said.

“You know Brittany ain’t going for that,”

“Let me handle her. I’m helping you; she's just jealous,” he said, picking up some shoes.

Randell and I stocked the entire store in 45 minutes, and Brittany cut her eyes at us. She really didn’t play with Randell because he didn’t give a fuck about putting her in her place. As she unlocked the doors, there was already a line out front. I hopped on register two and rang out as many people as possible.

“Did you find everything okay?” I asked the next customer

“Yes, I did,” he said.

“Good, good. Okay, your total is $565.48,” I said.

“I see you made it to work,” he said

"Do I know you?" I asked, finally paying attention to his handsome face.

"You ran right into me earlier," he said, showing off his beautiful smile.

"Oh, yeah, right I'm sorry again about that," I said, blushing.

"You good; I love when beautiful women run into me," he said, licking his lips.

"Cash or credit, and thank you," I said, blushing.

"Cash and your number," he said, handing me the money.

"Why would I do that?" I asked.

"Because I want to take you out, and from how you were running, you could use a day all about you," he said. I nodded, grabbed his receipt, and quickly wrote my number down.

"Have a good day," I said

"Now it's made, I'm Kelvin, by the way,"

"Wynter,"

"That's sexy, alright Wynter, I'll be calling,"

"Okay,"

"Enjoy your day, baby,"

"You too, bye," I said.

"Bitchhh, he is fine," Randell whispered.

"I know," I whispered back.

"Wynter, can you come here?" Brittany asked.

"Yeah," I said, walking over to her.

"You spent way too long with that customer. You know the rules. I'm going to have to write you up,"

"Whatever, Brittany," I said. At this point, I didn't care. Mr. Fine Ass had made my day, and even evil ass Brittany couldn't ruin that. I finished up my day at work and headed home. As soon as I got home, Kelvin texted me. He had me smiling all night and surprised me when he wanted to get on the phone together. We had a 6-hour conversation and fell asleep on the phone.

******

I had been texting Kelvin every day since he got my number, and I haven't stopped smiling, to say the least. It had only been a week, and I swear I could feel that he was perfect for me. We decided to go on a date Saturday night to Ruth Chris and then to a bar. Well, it was officially Saturday, and I was nervous as hell, so I called Randell for a pep talk.

"Helloooo bitch!" Randell yelled.

"Dell, I am so nervous,"

"Oh, that's right. Today is the day you getting fucked, right?"

"No, stupid, today is the date with Kelvin."

"Same thing bitch,"

"No, hoe, it's not."

"What are you nervous about? I mean yall been talking every day,"

"Right, I know, but it's our first date. I mean, wouldn't you be nervous?"

"Girl, I be fucking these niggas before the first date," he said, cracking gum.

"Randell!" I screamed, laughing.

"What? You know it's no shame in my game,"

"That I do know,"

"So, what are you wearing?"

"I was thinking maybe a dress and some heels,"

"Bitch get sexy! Where like those cute ass white flare pants you got with a white crop top and them gold Chanel sandals I got you for Christmas,"

"What kind of accessories?"

"Umm, do gold. As a matter of fact, let me see the outfit on," he said face, timing me.

"Randell, don't have on any clothes,"

"Wynter I am a gay man. I don't care about you being naked; I won't be moved, trust me," he said, laughing. I answered the FaceTime call and propped it on my dresser.

"Okay, girl, it's giving slim, thick," he said, snapping his finger. I laughed and got the outfit he talked about out of the closet.

I put the outfit on and stood in front of the camera.

"Yess bitchh, now wear that white purse you got, and you're all set,"

"What would I do without you?"

"Look a hot fucking mess. You look good, friend, I swear," he said, clapping.

"Thank you. You need to be a stylist,"

“It’s on my list of things to do. You’ll always get styled for free, though,”

“Aww, thank you. I love you,”

“Love you too. Now about that pussy did you wax?”

“Randell!”

“What? That man is not trying to get lost in the forest,”

“For your information, he won’t be getting lost because he won’t be getting any. And for your information nigga, I stay waxed,”

“Okay, just making sure you’re ready,”

“Man gone,” I said laughing. I sprayed my perfume on me and picked up my phone. I noticed Kelvin had texted me while I was on the phone running my mouth to Randell.

Kelvin: You ready beautiful?

Me: Yes, I’ll be there in 20 minutes.

“Okay, I got to go. Thank you for helping me.”

“Okay, have fun, pop that pussy bye,” he said, hanging up. I couldn’t do anything but laugh. Randell was a fool and truly my closest friend. I walked to the mirror to take a quick view. I put some moisturizer in my hair to make my curls juicier. Once I played with it a bit, I grabbed everything I needed and headed out the door.

I left the house just in time so I wouldn't be late. Instead of taking the streets, I took the freeway to get there quicker. While driving, I saw a text from Kelvin come across the screen. I unlocked my phone and read the text as I got off at the exit.

Kelvin: Here, I hope I didn't keep you waiting.

I put my phone down as I made a right into the parking lot. I reversed into the parking spot and parked. I grabbed my phone and texted him back.

Me: Hey, I'm here.

Kelvin: Don't move. I'm coming to get you.

I put my phone down, looked at the entrance, and there he stood, looking finer than before. I beeped my horn so he would know which car, and he jogged over. I opened my door, and he held his hand out for me.

"Never touch that door again," he said, licking his lips.

"Okay," I said, smiling. Kelvin was fine as hell, standing at 6'4, had the prettiest chocolate complexion, a set of pearly white teeth, and his dread was twisted neatly,

"You look gorgeous," he said, taking my hand.

"Thank you. You look handsome yourself," I said as we walked to the door. We were seated, and a waiter immediately walked over and took our drink orders.

"So, Wynter, why someone as pretty as yourself single?"

"I mean, I've been focusing on work, to be honest. I have so many goals I would like to complete, but I guess I never paid attention to them. What about you?"

"I haven't found my queen. I want that old-school love, but I can't see anyone giving it to me yet. I think this generation doesn't know what real love is,"

"And what is it?" I said, raising my eyebrow.

"It's loving you at your worst. Even when we don't see eye to eye. Even when I may feel like I hate you, I still love, protect, provide for you, and make sure you are straight no matter what," he said, sipping his patron.

"And you're ready for that kind of commitment?"

" I mean, I'm here, ain't I," he said, smirking.

"Yes, we are here. But we are going slow, just getting to know each other," I said, sipping my drink.

"We can go as slow as you need, baby," he said, kissing my hand. For the remainder of the night, we ate, talked, and drank more shots of liquor. By the time we were done, we both were good and drunk. Kelvin followed me to my apartment, and I guess you could say Randell was right. I'm sure glad I keep up with my waxes. After that night, you couldn't keep us apart.

****

Waking up to Kelvin almost every day was a dream come true. I mean, he did everything a man should. He protected, provided, and nurtured me. When we weren't together, we were texting nonstop. Even Randell got less of my time, and you know his ass had something to say about it.

"Bitch where the fuck have you been? I know that dick ain't that good," he yelled over the phone.

“I’m sorry, friend, I have been laid up. Yes, the dick is for sure that good. But it will never come in between us ever,”

“Mmmhmm, well, let’s go out tonight then. We haven’t been out in so damn long,”

“Okay, I’m down. Kelvin is out of town on a work assignment anyway,”

“Wynter ain’t nobody asks you about your funky ass boyfriend,”

“I’m just saying, it’s me and you tonight. No distractions,” I said, laughing.

“Okay bitch, we going to the Seven Eleven Lounge,”

“Randelllll,” I whined. Randell knew I hated clubs with a passion. I would much rather have preferred a nice little bar or something.

“I don’t want to hear none of that shit. You owe me because you’ve been missing in action,”

“Okay, okay, I’ll go,”

“And look cute too. Don’t be trying to wear no jeans, a T-shirt and tennis shoes,”

"Oh, bitch you know me so well. Okay, I won't," I said, laughing.

"Okay, I'll pick you up in about an hour,"

"Okay, I'll be ready," I said, hanging up.

I hopped up off my bed and went to my closet. I knew I had to dress my best when it came to Randell. He wouldn't let me out of the house if I didn't. I pulled out my multicolored leggings with the tie-up shirt to match. I was getting a little thicker since Kelvin had been feeding me, so I knew I would fill that shit out nicely. I grabbed my silver strapped heels, along with my silver handbag and some silver accessories. I went into the bathroom and removed my curly hair from my silk bonnet. The curls bounced down my back and framed my face. I was so happy. I had just rolled it up a few days prior, so it looked fresh.

I washed my face and decided on a fresh face today. I put on my clothes and heels when Randell rang my doorbell. I hurried to the door and opened it.

"Oh, bitch you look great," he said.

"You too!" I said. Randell wasn't the type to dress like a woman. He wore men's clothing tighter, and his makeup and accessories were on point. I let him in and closed the door. Once I turned around, I heard him scream and then fall to the ground.

“Bitch, what the fuck is wrong with you?” I said.

“Bitch, that man laying big daddy pipe, have you seen your ass and hips?” he said, still laid out.

“Randelll, get up,” I said, laughing hysterically.

“Unt uh, not until you tell me if he has a gay brother,”

“No, he doesn’t,” I said, doubling over in laughter.

“What? What’s funny? Bitch I want my booty to grow too.” He said, getting off the floor.

“You are sick as hell,”

“Not as sick as that ass bitch you thick,” he said as he followed me to my room. I put on the rest of my stuff and grabbed my purse, keys, and phone.

“Let’s go,” he said.

“My car or yours?”

“Mines because I’m dropping you off and going to my boo's house around the corner after,”

“Okay, cool,” I said as we walked out the door, and I locked it behind us. The ride to Seven-Eleven was quick because I lived about 10 minutes away. Randell had already purchased a section for us before we got there. We parked and walked into the club like we owned the place.

Seven Eleven was one of the city's hottest clubs; tonight, everyone and their mama seemed to be there.

“I’m glad we got the section because it’s packed, and your feet would be barking!” Randell yelled over the music.

“Me too,” I yelled back. He took my hand and guided me to our section. One thing about Randell is that he always protected me. He was gay, but he could stand toe to toe with some of the biggest niggas. Him being in boxing at a young age played a big part in that. We made it to our section, and the waitress instantly came over, took our drink order, and asked if we were ordering food.

“We drinking Hennessey tonight, sis,” Randell said.

“Randell, now you know I can’t do no damn dark,” I warned. Dark liquor always made me sick or sleepy.

“Shut up, you’ll be fine,” he waved me off. The waitress left and returned with our bottles, chasers, and cups. Randell poured our first shot, and it was on from there. I was having the time of my life. I was keeping it cute for my man’s sake, but I wouldn’t lie and say I didn’t enjoy the attention I was getting.

“The niggas is up in here tonight!” Randell yelled and started twerking.

“Now you know-“

“Blah blah blahhh, we know already,” he said playfully, rolling his eyes.

“I got to go to the bathroom really quickly,” he said.

“You want me to walk with you?”

“Of course not. Stay here. I’ll be right back,” he said, walking towards the bathroom. I sat and sipped on my 5th cup of Hennessey slowly because I was feeling the effects of the liquor, and I didn’t need to be asleep or sick. I was actually enjoying myself but was missing my man, so I texted him.

Me: Bae, wyd? I miss you.

I hit send, and the phone must have been in his hand because he had responded one minute later.

Bae: I miss you more, beautiful. Man in this hotel tired as hell. They worked me like a slave today.

Me: I wish I was there with you.

Bae: Me too. I miss everything about you. When I get back I'm taking you shopping.

Me: Okay, but I want to do something nice for you too.

Bae: You can, but just being you is a big enough gift.

Me: Ohh, you must want some sloppy head when I see you!!

Bae: You must want to ride my face when I see you!

Me: I sure do!

Bae: Say less, I'm coming home tomorrow.

Me: I thought you had to stay long?

Bae: Nope, we're done early, so I can come home to you.

Me: Okay.

Bae: wyd?

Before I could respond, Randell came back into the section, yelling my name.

“What?”

“Bitch, your nigga is here?”

“What nigga?” I yelled as my heart sped up.

“Bitch Kelvin, and he in the section with some bitch on his lap,”

“Randell, he is in Ohio! He isn’t here. It must be a look like,”

“Wynter, I know what that nigga looks like.” He yelled. I could tell he was serious at this point.

“Show me,” I said. I knew Randell was mistaken until we walked to the back and saw Kelvin in the section. His phone was in his hand while the girl sat on his lap. He texted and then put the phone down and palmed her ass. My phone instantly alerted me of a text. My heart sped up, my palms got sweaty, and I was pissed the fuck off. I stood there as the girl turned her head, and he tongued her down. That was it for me; I stormed right over there.

“Wynter!” I heard Randell say, but I was seeing red, and he had me fucked up.

“Is this what the fuck you doing? You lying ass nigga!” I screamed. Kelvin's eyes widened as he looked shocked to see me.

“Who is this?” the girl asked.

“Who am I Kelvin. You got this hoe on your lap! Kissing and shit! But you in the hotel?!” I screamed.

“Watch your mouth,” the hoe said.

“Aye, this ain’t what you want, little mama! That’s her man the fuck,” I heard Randell say behind me.

“Baby, Wynter, please look,” he said, moving so the girl could get up.

“Nah nigga, I don’t want to hear shit. You fucking played me. Why, though?” I said, and my voice cracked. I could feel the tears welling up in my eyes.

“Nah, not here,” Randell said, grabbing my hand and rushing me out of the club.

“Wynter! Wait, baby!” Kelvin said behind me. We rushed out of the club and straight to Randell’s car.

He unlocked the door, and I slid in; that’s when the tears finally fell.

“Wynter, please talk to me,” Kelvin said, opening the door.

“Nigga, get your hands off my fucking door,” Randell yelled.

“Aye, my nigga this between me and my bitch! I don’t know who the fuck you talking to.”

“I’m talking to you,” Randell said, opening his door,

“No, stop y'all,” I said, getting out.

“Man, move so we can go nigga. You fucked up,” Randell yelled, getting his boxing stance.

“This between us like I said, and I ain’t going no fucking where until she talks to me,” Kelvin yelled, pulling up his pants.

“Oh, you not?” Randell said, walking up, and I jumped in front of them both.

“Fucking stop!” I screamed and started crying.

“Bae, please, talk to me,” she said, grabbing my hand.

“Get your hands off her,” Randell yelled.

“Randell, just go sit in the car real quick,”

“Bitch I know-“

“Just please, Randell, I’m coming,” I said.

“Okay, bitch because you know,”

“She knows what nigga?” Kelvin said.

“Randell, for me, please,” I begged. He nodded and slid into the driver's seat.

“What?”

“Bae, I swear I was drunk, man I’m sorry,”

“Is that all you have to say? You drunk? Nigga get the fuck on,” I yelled

“Man, please don’t do me like that, Wynter man. I love you,”

“Love? So love made you lie and kick it with another bitch?”

“No man, that shit don’t mean shit,”

“Bye,” I said

“Please let me just come over tonight,”

“Hell naw, you just kissed that hoe in the mouth the fuck you think we doing? It’s over for you and me. Fuck you,” I said and got in the car. As soon as the door closed, Randell pulled off. I couldn't believe the shit that went on. I never felt like Kelvin would do anything to hurt me. I trusted him, and he lied.

2

Depressed wasn't even the word for how I felt about Kelvin. It had been only two weeks since the incident, and I was a wreck. His lying like that to my face made me feel like I was hit with a damn truck. No matter what I did or how I felt, I still got up and took my ass to work. Today was no different. When my alarm clock went off, I looked at it. I had already been up for hours. I pressed the button and got up. I took care of my hygiene and took my ass to work. When I walked in, the first person I saw was Brittany.

"She gone get her ass beat today if she gets on bullshit. I am not in the mood," I thought.

I walked right past her and headed for the employee break room.

"Hey, Dell," I said, spotting him sitting at the table. I put my things in the locker, and he stared at me.

"Why are you looking at me like that?" I asked.

"Because bitch who died?"

"What are you talking about?"

"Did someone die?"

"No, Randell, why would you say that?"

"Because bitch you look horrible. Your hair is in that crusty-ass matted ponytail. Your eyes are pussy as hell, and not to mention look at your uniform,"

"I ain't in the mood to be cute,"

"Wynter, you don't ever let a nigga affect you that bad that you are letting yourself go,"

"But Randell, he hurt my feelings," I said with tears.

"I get that, baby, but you look like shit. This ain't you. I don't think he is right for you because you have changed who you are, my love. The old you would never leave the house like this for anyone."

"I know. I think I fell for him fast, and I just can't seem to understand why," I said.

"Wynter, you are one of the baddest bitches in this city, me being number one of course. Anyway, you can have any nigga you want. Fuck that nigga"

"One thing about it you gone find a way to insert yourself," I said laughing.

"But I am serious, you're my best friend, I hate to see you like this over him. Shit, you should've called up the old niggas you had by now," he said.

"When I get with someone Randell, you know that I don't be dealing with no other niggas."

"And that's the problem, you aren't supposed to let your niggas go for any nigga until a solid commitment,"

"I thought we had one,"

"Well, you thought wrong shit, and until it's solidified, you keep your niggas,"

"I don't even know if I want a new nigga,"

"Even if you don't, that doesn't mean look the way you do,"

"Okay, I get it. I will get myself together,"

"Not only that, but bitch we going outside,"

"Randell!"

"No, ain't no, Randell, we need to get you out of that damn house. So on break, we gone find you an out and get cute,"

"Okay," I said, smiling.

Leave it up to Randell to make me feel better. I knew he was right. Shit, Kelvin had played himself, and instead of sulking in my misery, I needed to snap out that shit.

We left the break room and started our shift. Surprisingly, Brittany wasn't in her mood. She didn't bother us at all. Randell and I were stocking the shelves when I heard a voice behind me.

"Wynter?" he said. The sound of his voice sent chills down my spine.

"Oh hell naw," Randell said. I turned around, and Kelvin stood with sadness in his eyes and a bouquet of roses.

"What are you doing here?" I asked.

"I came here to apologize. I am so sorry for hurting you. I never meant for it to go down like that. I messed up, and I will never do anything to hurt you again," he said, handing me the flowers.

"Kelvin, I appreciate the flowers, but I do not want to talk to you,"

"Just give me another chance. I promise I won't ever play in your face like that again," he begged.

"Kelvin, I'm sorry, but no,"

“I’m never gonna stop trying and I do really love you, Wynter,”

“Okay,” I said. Kelvin kissed my cheek and then left the store.

“Ohh bitch, you standing on business. I am proud of you,” Randell said.

“I know,” I said, looking down at the flowers.

“You going back, ain’t you bitch,”

“Dell, I-“

“Come, Wynter, it’s me, just tell me straight up,”

“Now you know I am,” I said.

“Well, shit, no judgment, but make him wait. Make him think you ain’t so that nigga won’t ever play with you again,”

“I am,”

“Second chances are okay, Wynter, it’s the third and fourth ones I don’t fuck with. Let that nigga know who the fuck you are,”

“Period,” I said.

“We're still going out tonight, though.”

“Alright bet, we will go on our break,” I said.

I was back to my bubbly self now that Randell cheered me up, but honestly, it was because of Kelvin, too. Yes, he had been trying to call, but his showing up made me think he wanted to fix us. I stood firm with him this time, and some ground rules would be laid out. But before I did that, I was kicking it. Kelvin was gone; understand not to play with me. After work, we went shopping and then headed to my house. I took care of my hygiene before Randell started glamming me up.

A bad bitch wasn't the word for how I felt when he was done. My hair was in a fresh 30-inch wig. Randell pressed it bone straight for me. I applied a light beat before slipping on my outfit for the night. I was a very conservative girl; however, I told Randell he could pick the outfit, and I wouldn't make a fuss. This nigga chose a see-through black mesh body suit. The breast and stomach parts weren't mesh; they were the same cloth of shapewear that pushed up my breast. The back was completely see-through, so I was told not to wear panties. I bought some shark boot dups and a black purse to match.

I had to buy a thong. I can't lie when I looked in the mirror, I looked so damn good. The outfit hugged my body so tight that when I turned around, my ass looked bigger.

"Ohh bitch that's what the fuck I'm talking about," he said.

"Do you think I need a jacket or something?" I asked.

"If you put on a jacket, I'm gonna pop your ass. You look bad as hell. Spray you some perfume, and let's go. I got us a section."

"Okay, okay, I'm coming," I said, spraying Good Girl.

I locked up my house, and we took Randell's jeep instead of mine. We rode to the club, listening to music to hype me up. He handed me a patron shot, and we pre-gamed on the way. When we pulled up, the club was packed.

"I knew I should've bought a jacket," I mumbled.

"Get your fine ass out of my car. Live a little; we all know you go back to your man, but have some fun first," he said, getting out of the car.

Randell actually matched me. He had on a mesh see-through shirt, leather pants, and some cute ass boots. He paired his outfit with black sunglasses and a black clutch purse. His makeup was beat down, and he had just got a fresh haircut. We walked over to the front door, and Randell gave him a look and our confirmation number.

“I know he ain’t fucking the doorman,” I thought.

“Thanks, Big Mike,” he said sexily.

“Yea, he's fucking the doorman,” I thought to myself, smiling.

When we got to the section, two girls came over to take our bottles and food orders.

“I’ll pay for it since you got the section. Babe, what’s the total?” I said, taking some money out of my purse.

“Baby, put it away unless you're tipping that much money. It’s handled. Now, my love, bring us bottles of water, like 3 a piece as well.” He said, handing her $50. I followed suit and gave the other one $50 as well.

“Thank you, it will be right out.” She said, smiling. When they left, I bobbed to Sexy Red’s “Get It Sexy.”

“Bitch, you fucking the doorman?” I asked, scooting over and whispering into Randell’s ear.

"Hell yea, that's my main nigga baby. We ain't paying for any of this. He paid for it all, he gave me the money for it. We good shit paid in full, and he gave me more than enough," he said, smacking his lips and clapping his hands.

"Oh bitch you be going to town on that nigga," I said, laughing.

"Bitch I be going downtown, small town, big town, a big rich town, all that shit. He loves me," he said, and I fell out laughing.

About 10 minutes later, our bottles, water, and chasers came out. We ordered patron and Casamigos. We poured our drinks, and baby, by shot number 4, I was twerking on the couch. We were having the time of our lives, and I was good and drunk. By drink number 7, baby, I was the life of the party.

"Oh my gawddd bitch look at the door," Randell said with his hand over his mouth. I turned around and saw Kelvin walking in with 3 of his friends.

"I don't give a fuck. I'm kicking it," I said. I turned back around and grabbed the bottle to pour me another drink.

“Ohhh bitch that liquor got you feeling yourself, and I hope you got some courage juice because he coming right towards your ass,” he said, laughing.

I sat and crossed my legs as I sipped on my 8th drink. I knew I ain’t need shit else, but I was having a damn time. I watched out the corner of my eye as Kelvin walked in front of the section. He lifted the rope and slid next to me on the couch. He leaned in and kissed my neck while sniffing me. He smelled like Hennessy, and he was drunk as hell. I had never seen him drunk, so I was amused.

“Damn baby, you look so fucking good,” he said.

“Thank you, you look good too,” I said. My eyes were low as hell. He licked his lips, grabbed my neck, and kissed me. My pussy started throbbing as soon as he let my lips go.

“Stand up, show me that shit you got on,” he said, holding my hand in the hair to help me up. I stood up and then turned around so he could get a full view of my ass. He smacked my ass, and I looked back at him before sitting down.

“You coming home with me tonight.” He said.

“I’ll think about it,” I said, laughing.

“I didn’t ask, I’m telling you, you're coming home with me tonight,” he said again.

“Okay, Daddy,” I said softly.

“Say that shit again,” he said.

“Okay, Daddy,” I said again, biting my lip.

“You better stop before we leave right now,” he warned.

“Let’s leave in an hour, baby,” I said.

“Alright, I’m a go tell my niggas, and then I’ll be back over here,”

“Okay, that’s cool, but you can kick it over there if you want,” I said.

“You see the shit you got on? I wish the fuck I would,” he said, standing up. As soon as he left, Randell rushed over to me and damn near knocked me off the couch.

“Bitch, you getting fucked tonight. Yall was damn near about to fuck over here! It’s the ass slaps for me,” he said twerking.

“Damn, my ass folded,” I said, slurring.

“Yes, your drunk ass did, I just knew you would early too. But bitch, the way he was looking at you and the way yall look tonight, I would've too," he said. Before I could respond, Kelvin walked back over.

"Come here real quick. I got to get something from the car," he said. Confused, I threw my last shot back, grabbed my purse, and told Randell I would be back.

"Mmhm," he said and continued to dance. Kelvin grabbed my hand and walked me out of the club. When we returned to his truck, he opened the door for me, and I got in.

He got into the driver's seat and turned on the AC.

"I thought you said you needed to get something," I said.

"I do take that off real quick. Let me eat your pussy," he said.

"Bae, right now?" I said, taking my shoes off.

"Now, can't nobody see us, these windows tinted to the darkest legal level," he said, letting his seat back. I hurried up, stripped out the body suit, and sat back down.

"What you doing? Get the fuck up here," he said, licking his lips. I put one leg on the side of his seat while he helped lift me higher onto his face. His seat was back to the back seat, so I could sit comfortably. As soon as I was comfortable, he started attacking my clit.

“Ohhh shit,” I moaned as he flickered his tongue across my clit. He reached up and grabbed my nipples and massaged them as I rolled my hips to the beat of his tongue.

I started to gently suck on my clit as I put my hand on the window to catch my balance.

“Ohhh fuck, damn,” I moaned as he licked my pussy faster.

“Oh shit, oh, I’m about to cum,” I moaned fucking his face.

“Mmmhmm,” he moaned as he licked faster.

“Ohh, what the fuck, ohhh right there,” I moaned louder.

“I’m cumming, I’m cumming,” I moaned while shaking as I felt my sweet cum slide out my pussy and into his mouth. He licked up every drop before helping back into the seat. At this point, I was tired and ready to sleep. He helped me put my outfit back on and shoes.

"I ain't done with you. Let's go,"

"Okay, let me go tell Randell," I said.

"I'm about to go tell these niggas I'm gone, and I'll tell Randell too," he said.

I really didn't have any energy, so I agreed. I pulled out my phone and sent him a text anyway. He replied that he already knew and was leaving with the doorman anyway. He told me he loved me and to be safe. The liquor had taken into effect, and I couldn't keep my eyes open. Before I knew it, I fell asleep with my head on the window.

****

It had been two months since the night at the club. Kelvin and I were inseparable. Shit, I basically lived at his house. I was damn near a house. I cooked every night, went to work during the day, and fucked him on command. I was actually enjoying the life I started with him. Kelvin had been showering me with love and gifts since he fucked up. I mean, he was even paying bills at my house and his. Shit was a dream. But, everything that glitters ain't gold.

It was Saturday, my day off, which was rare for me because it was one of the busiest days at the store.

I woke up to Kelvin's side of the bed empty. He had gone out the night prior, and I was too tired to join. I grabbed my cell phone off the nightstand and dialed his number. It went straight to voicemail. I started to get worried because his phone had never died. Something clicked in my mind, and I called his phone private.

"Hello?" he answered.

"Nigga did you block me?" I yelled.

"Wynter?"

"Who the fuck else is calling,"

"No, baby, I was just confused because you called me private,"

"That's because your phone went to voicemail when I called from my damn number. Now it's mysteriously ringing,"

"Babe, my phone was dead; it just cut on. I'm just now leaving Wayne's house. His ass got too drunk, I had to drive him home, and I fell asleep on the couch,"

"Why didn't you call me and tell me you weren't coming home?"

"Babe, I was drunk my damn self. We bought the bar last night. I told you to come with me because I knew I would've had an excuse,"

"Okay, Kelvin, when are you coming home?"

"Baby, didn't you hear me? I said I was on my way and would also stop and get us some breakfast. Since you are off, we can have a lazy day in bed. I'll order out since you've been cooking every night, and we can cuddle. We can eat whatever you want to eat and whatever snacks you want too."

"Mmm, that sounds fun, okay baby, see you when you get here. You know what I want for breakfast?"

"Meat lovers' omelet, loaded hash browns, Texas toast, side of ham and sausage with apple juice,"

"You know me so well. I love you,"

"Of course I do, beautiful, I love you too," he said, hanging up.

I felt better now that I had talked to Kelvin, but as I got up to take care of my hygiene, I couldn't shake this feeling I had. It was like in the pit of my gut, I knew some bullshit was going on, but I ignored it. I took a shower, brushed my teeth, and did my skincare. When I was done, I put my hair in a bun before applying coconut oil to my skin. I put on one of his oversized tee shirts and laid back in bed.

I heard Kelvin's door open and shut when I got in good with one of my shows. He walked into the room, held up the food bag, and walked over to give me a kiss. The scent of Dior for men mixed with Good Girl filled my nostrils.

“What the fuck?” I thought.

“Did you have fun at the strip club, bae?” I asked.

“Hell yea, that shit was a movie,” he said, putting the food down. I side-eyed him because he didn’t go to know damn strip club. He said he was going to 7220, which was a downtown club.

“That’s all you went to last night?”

“Yeah, why are you asking so many questions, baby?”

“No reason,” I said, smiling.

He smiled back while taking off his clothes and heading for the shower. He placed his phone on the charger and entered the bathroom, closing the door behind him.

I could’ve broken my pinky toe trying to get to his phone. I knew Kelvin’s code because I saw him put it in many times. I put the code in and went straight to the messages. I saw Wayne first and then an unsaved number. When I clicked on Wayne’s first, my blood started boiling. This nigga told Wayne to say he was with him if he called and asked. Of course, Wayne agreed. I then went to the unsaved number and read those.

My blood pressure started to rise, and I felt a rage I never felt before. He had a date last night. Then went and spent the night with the bitch. I wanted to beat her ass because she knew about me based on the messages and his ass. After all, why the fuck are you playing with me. I took pictures of all the messages and placed his phone back on the charger. I grabbed the food bag and took my food out. Let me be honest; I knew I wasn't leaving Kelvin; the way he fucked me, ate my pussy, and catered to me had me sprung. I had never had a nigga do what he was doing.

I knew I was being stupid, but shit, I was in love with his ass. Oh, but I was furious as fuck. I couldn’t get him fucking another bitch out of my mind as I ate. Shit, I even started to feel nauseous. He had my head gone, and I was wide open to him.

“What the fuck can I do to make him faithful. Like, is it me? Why can’t he be faithful?” I thought as I ate.

Once I got done eating, Kelvin came out of the bathroom looking so fucking good. My pussy instantly started throbbing.

“Bitch stop,” I thought.

“So, babe, you were with Wayne, right?”

“Wynter, what’s up? You keep asking me the same question,” he said, putting on his briefs.

“Because you’re fucking lying, Kelvin!” I screamed.”

“Man, Wynter, I don’t have time for this!”

“You did fucking lie! I saw your messages nigga. You were with a bitch!” I yelled.

“Wynter, why are you going through my phone?”

“Nigga are you serious? You literally cheated on me last night, and that’s all you have to say?!” I yelled with tears streaming down my face.

“Bae, don’t cry, I am so sorry. Man, I've been going through shit. My grandmother was in the hospital, and my father wasn’t a real man to me growing up. I ain't never had a woman like you before Wynter. I'm used to bitches shitting on me, and I guess I'm damaged. I be trying to hurt before I can get hurt. Please, baby, don't leave me! I promise I will go to therapy. I will really work on this shit I got going on. I want to be the best man I can be for you. Wynter, I see you as my wife and my kid's mother. I promise, baby, if you give me another chance, I won't ever do this shit again. Please don't leave me, Wynter," he said with tears in his eyes.

I felt so bad because I had no idea his grandmother was sick or that he didn't have a father figure. I mean, how do you know how to treat a woman if you weren't taught? Kelvin walked over to me and pulled me into a hug as the tears streamed down my cheeks.

"Stop crying, baby. I promise I won't hurt you again," he said, kissing my forehead. I nodded my head because I honestly wanted to believe him. But like I said before, it wasn't like I was leaving.

3

My mood had been down since Kelvin cheated again. We were in an okay place, but at the same time, I knew he wouldn't be faithful; I just wasn't willing to lose him either. I decided to get dressed and see my parents. My parents were the best parents in the world. I loved my mom so much, but I was a daddy's girl to the core. Since I started dating Kelvin, I hadn't seen them in months. Not even a call. I was slipping. I took care of my hygiene, through my hair in a bun and through on a cute little jogging suit. I slipped my feet into some sandals, grabbed my purse and keys, and headed out the door.

I jumped in my car and headed to my parents' house. I was relieved to see both their cars in the driveway when I arrived. I wanted to surprise them, so I didn't call first. I parked behind my dad's truck and got out. I used my key to open the door and didn't see anyone in the foyer. I walked to the kitchen and spotted them listening to old-school R&B while dancing. I leaned on the wall and smiled. This was the kind of love you only read about in books. 30 years was a long time to be with one person through thick and thin. As my father turned my mother around, she jumped when she saw me.

“Wynter, you scared the hell out of me,” she said, holding her chest.

“I’m sorry I missed y'all,” I said, laughing.

“Come here, my baby. I missed you. Where have you been?” my mom said, walking around and kissing my cheek before pulling me into a tight hug.

“I’ve been working, mama, while on break,”

“Come here, princess,” my dad said with open arms. I stepped out of my mom’s embrace and hugged my father tightly. He kissed my forehead before releasing me.

“So, how are you?” my mom asked, getting water from the fridge and then sitting at the table.

“I am good mommy, working like crazy and preparing to go back to school,”

“You’ve always been so smart. Don’t work too hard, though. It looks like you have lost a lot of weight,” she said.

“Yeah, I have been stressing a little,”

"If you need some money or anything, you know we are here, baby," my mom said.

"I know, Mommy, I am fine. I promise I've just been working," I lied.

"Well, listen, I need to run to the store for dinner; how about you spend the night with us? We can bake some cookies, eat, and have family time," she said excitedly.

"Yes, I would love that," I smiled.

"Okay, well, I was gonna make something quick, but I'm gonna make a feast for us," she said. My mom grabbed her purse, keys, and my dad's card and kissed us both before heading out the door.

"So, you want to tell me the truth?" my dad asked.

"What do you mean?"

"You're a bad liar, Wynter. You can't fool me. You've always been able to fool Nancy, but not your ole man," he said.

"My relationship is a little rocky, that's all," I said.

"Is he hitting you?"

"Oh no, he would never,"

"Disrespecting you?"

"No,"

"Well, then it can be fixed, I think. You're special, Wynter; don't let any man bring your mood down. If he isn't treating you right, leave. If he isn't providing leave. There are plenty of young men who would love to be with you. You're smart, you'll make the right decision," he said.

"How you know daddy,"

"Shit, you, my daughter, then my genes. Hell, in my day, I was something else. But I changed for you and your mama. If he's right, whatever he's doing, he will too,"

"Thank you, Daddy," I said, getting up and hugging him.

"Good, now let's play uno, I know you love that game."

"Now, Daddy, you know you can't beat me," I said, laughing.

"Girl, I taught you how to play. This my shit," he said, causing me to laugh. My father and I played UNO for hours. You would've thought I had been gone for years the way my mother was cooking. She made mac and cheese, string beans, yams, baked ham, ribs, potato salad, deviled eggs, rolls, and greens. We threw down. By the time I was done eating, all I wanted to do was sleep.

We decided to finish off with a movie night. My dad sat on the couch, my mom sat cuddled under him, and I laid my head on her lap. I felt so much better. This was what I needed. My spirits were lifted again. By 10PM, I was in my old bed, knocked out with the biggest smile. One thing about it is that a parent's love could heal anything.

The following day, when I woke up, my parents begged me to stay again during breakfast.

"Just one more night," my mom said. I felt like shit because I had been away so long.

"Mom, I promise I will be back. How about we make it our business to have weekly family dinners. How does that sound?"

"Perfect, that sounds perfect," she said.

"So what day will that be?" my dad asked.

"How about Sunday, just like Soul Food,"

"Sunday it is," my mom said.

"I like Sunday, so we can watch football during the season, too," my dad said.

"Yes, we will, and I promise never to miss a Sunday," I said.

"I'm a hold you to that," my father said. I kissed my parents goodbye and made my way to Kelvin's house. I knew Kelvin and I needed to talk officially to get our relationship on the right track. When I arrived, I used my key to get in and walked through the living room to the bedroom.

"Hey babe, how was your parent's house?" he asked, sitting up.

"It was so nice, but I want to talk with you,"

"Okay, let's talk," he said.

'Kelvin, are you happy? I mean, really happy? The constant cheating is a bit much, and I know I don't deserve it," I said.

"You're right, you don't, and I am so sorry Wynter. You're so special to me. I don't know why I made those mistakes, but I can tell you that I promise I won't again. I love you so much. I see my future with you and only you,"

" I love you too, babe. I just want us to be okay," I said, sitting on the bed.

"And we will, beautiful," Kelvin said, getting up and walking towards me.

"We will, we will be amazing parents, and you will be an amazing wife. You will never have to work; shit, if you want, you can quit now," he said, causing me to laugh.

"Really?" I said.

"Yes, I want to make you happy because making you happy makes me happy. How about we do a mini getaway? Go to a resort or something. I want to make you feel like the queen you are," he said.

"Yes, I would love that. Let me look up some! Where at?" I squealed with excitement.

"Let's do Miami." He said, winking at me.

"Thank you, baby," I said, hugging him. That showed me he listened to me when I would rant. I also talked about how I would love to go to Miami.

"I love this man so much," I thought as I looked up flights and resorts.

By the end of the night, Kelvin booked everything I wanted, and my jaws were locking. He deserved it. He was really showing me that he was changing for me. Yes, he made some mistakes, but it was hard to resist. He was everything I dreamed of.

The next day, we left for Miami. We got on an early flight, and Kelvin told me not to pack anything but essentials because he was paying for everything when we touched down. After the 3-hour flight, we were in Mami and checking into the Fontainebleau 5-star Hotel.

"This is so beautiful," I said, looking around.

"Just like you," Kelvin said as he hugged me.

"This weekend is exactly what we needed," I said, putting my arms around his neck.

"Why don't you move in with me officially?"

"What?"

"I mean, you are always at my house anyway. If you want to keep your place, I'll pay the rent. I just think it will make us stronger." He said, kissing my lips.

"Of course, I'll move in,"

"Alright, so when we get back, you can go home for a few days to pack up, and I'll have the movers get your stuff,"

“I love you so much, you know that.

“I love you more; I’m just trying to show you that I am ready to be 100% committed to you,” he said, releasing me from the hug. I smiled as we walked hand in hand to the counter to check in our room. Kelvin kept his promise and took me shopping for the weekend. I loved every minute of it. He carried my bags everywhere, and I felt like a true queen. When we got done shopping, we fucked and took a nap because he said he had a surprise for dinner.

We woke up a few hours later, took care of our hygiene, and got dressed.

“You look so good,” he said as I admired myself in the mirror. My hair was pinned up in loose curls that framed my face. My makeup was light due to the Miami heat. I wore a long pink boho beach dress with silver strappy heels, the bracelet and diamond necklace Kelvin bought me, and the matching clutch. He wore loose beach pants and a matching shirt, showing off his chiseled chest.

“Don’t you look real Greek Godish,” I said,

“Come on before we're late,” he said, laughing. We walked hand in hand through the hotel lobby and out the door. A black car awaited us, and the driver opened the door as Kelvin helped me inside.

We rode through the beautiful city until we reached a dark parking lot.

“Where the hell are we?”

"You trust me?” he asked.

“Yes,”

“Okay, well, trust me, baby,” he said, getting out of the car. He opened my door and led me to some steps. When I looked down, I saw the beach.

“Take your shoes off, and I’ll carry them while walking across the beach,” he said. He helped me remove my shoes, and we walked down the stairs onto the beach. After about 5 minutes of walking, I saw lights flickering. As we got closer, I noticed a candlelight dinner with a red carpet, a waiter, flowers, and a violinist playing soft music.

“Oh my God, this is beautiful,” I said, covering my mouth as tears formed in my eyes. Kelvin took my hand and walked me over to my seat. He pulled out my chair and stood before me as I sat down.

“I am so sorry for the things I have put you through. You are the only woman for me. I wanna give you this ring. As a promise that I am committed to you, and the only time you take it off is when I give you your engagement ring," he said, kneeling and putting it on my finger.

All I could do was nod because I was now in full-blown tears. Nobody had ever made me feel like Kelvin had before. I felt like I had found my soulmate.

"Thank you," I said between sobs as he kissed me and took his seat.

The waiter bought our seafood food, and we devoured it. After eating, we returned to the hotel and devoured each other. My man, my man, my man.

4

I felt so much better after returning home from our trip. Kelvin wasn't playing when he said he was sending me home to pack what I wanted and move in. I did just that. It had been two days since I saw my man. We agreed it would take me four days to pack, but I wanted to surprise him in the middle of it. I went to Kelvin's house to surprise him and decorate it. He had shown me such a beautiful time in Miami that I also wanted to show my appreciation. I felt like a whole new woman. I listened to some good old 90s R&B as I drove down the expressway. Today felt like a beautiful day. I made it to his condo and locked up my car. I opened the door and immediately stopped in my tracks. I dropped my purse and phone on the couch while observing the scene.

Heels, clothes, and shoes were all over the living room. There was weed and multiple bottles of liquor on the floor. I tiptoed through his massive condo until I came to the master bedroom. The door was wide open. There laid Kelvin and some bitch cuddled up together, sleeping peacefully.

I didn't react, I couldn't. I stared at them as my anger rose to a level I had never experienced. I stared until a light bulb went off in my head. I went to the living room closet and pulled out his brass knuckles. I placed them on my hands and marched back to the room. I walked over to his side of the bed and punched him as hard as I could. I saw red.

"Oh my god!" the girl screamed.

"Wynter, wtf!" He yelled.

I continued to punch him in the face as he tried to fight back. If it was any regular punch, I knew Kelvin would've been able to get up. But the brass knuckles caused him to bleed more and more with every hit. He couldn't react the way he wanted to because I punched his ass out of his sleep. Blood squirted on my face with every blow.

"You're gonna kill him!" the girl screamed, getting out of bed and running out of the room.

When I heard that, I stopped. Kelvin was still shielding his bloody face. I looked down at my hands and saw bruises and blood all over them. I looked at my shirt, and it was covered in his blood. I looked at the bed and was mortified.

“Oh my God!” I cried. I stepped back and threw the brass knuckles off my hands. I slid down the walls, smacking my head.

“Fuck, fuck. fuck!” I screamed.

Kelvin mustered enough strength to get out of bed and stumble out of the room. The girl let out a loud scream before comforting him.

What the fuck did I do, I blacked out.

I stared into space as I heard sirens coming towards the condo. Tears streamed down my face, and I couldn’t move. I couldn’t. I was stuck. I heard the officers and paramedics arrive, but I was stuck. I heard them ask where I was and if I was armed. The next thing I saw was the officer asking me if I could walk or talk. I nodded yes. He stood me up, and they placed my bloody hands behind my back.

As the officers walked me out of the condo, people recorded me and snapped pictures. I hung my head, not knowing what my fate would be. As I was in the car, I looked out the window at the sky and silently prayed that my parents would forgive me for everything I had just done.

The drive to the police station was slow. Everything felt like it was moving in slow motion. I almost felt like I was about to faint. The voices on the radio were deep and slow.

"What the fuck did I do?" I thought.

"How the fuck did I snap like this?

"Oh my God, what about school? Randell, My family," I thought.

My chest heaved up and down as I started having trouble breathing,

"You okay back there?" He asked, turning around. I didn't respond to him; tears streamed down my cheeks as I returned to reality.

"Oh my God!" I cried. I was broken. I had finally realized the magnitude of my crime. I had let a nigga push me to the limit. The police car sped through the parking lot and into a garage. He quickly got out and opened my door.

"Are you okay?" he asked again. I looked up at him as the tears didn't stop. I dropped my head and shook it no.

"Are you in pain? Can you breathe? Do you need medical?" he asked, lifting my chin.

I shook my head no.

“Hey, hey, it’s bad, yes, but you’re going to be okay. I will put in a word that you didn’t resist.” He said. I nodded as I placed my feet on the ground, and he helped me up.

I walked into the station and was immediately placed inside a room. After about 20 minutes, two police officers came in.

“Hello, I am detective Marshall; this is detective Lynn. You want to tell us what happened?”

“No, she doesn’t, not without me present. Can I have a moment with my client?” a woman asked, walking into the room. The two detectives looked at each other and walked out of the room.

“Okay, tell me what happened, Wynter. Your mom and dad sent me.”

“How did they know?”

“Apparently, your boyfriend called Randell and told him everything, and they immediately called me. Now, this is a tough case, Wynter, because you were at the scene of the crime with the weapon and have two witnesses, one being the victim. What happened, Wynter?” she said.

"I don't know," I said sobbing.

"Babe, you have to pull together and tell me what happened. They are already talking about giving you 10 years in prison. For that not to happen, I need you to tell me everything that happened." She said. I looked at her and realized she was right. I needed to get myself together; I knew I couldn't do 10 years, shit I didn't even know if I could do a year.

I inhaled deeply and told her everything she asked me and needed to know. She let me know that tomorrow, I would have a bond hearing.

"Will I be able to go home?"

"I will fight my hardest for a bond," she said, packing her bag.

"Okay," I said.

Two officers came back into the room and placed me back in cuffs before leading me out. I had several things to do to get booked. They took my picture, took possession of whatever I had, and documented it. They then made me remove my clothes and change into the inmate uniforms. They then took me back to my cell, where I was alone.

"Hey, can I get a phone call?" I asked.

“Yes,” the woman said. She took me to the phone, and I called my parents first.

“Please state your name, and we will try to connect your call,” the operator said.

“Wynter Lewis,” I said.

I waited for the phone to connect and heard my father’s voice.

“Baby girl,”

“Daddy, I am so sorry,” I said, sobbing.

“I know, baby, don’t say anything over this phone. Your mom and I will be there tomorrow as well for the bond hearing,”

“Okay, thank you so much,” I said, crying.

“Your mother is sleeping, and she is taking this so hard right now. She has been crying for a while. I got you and her, though. We will see you tomorrow, Princess. I love you so much,” he said.

“I love you too. I will see you tomorrow,” I said, hanging up.

“I just need one more call,” I said.

"Make it quick, Lewis. You're the only one in intake tonight, so you can do this, but it would be no other time," the officer said.

"Okay, thanks," I said, dialing Randell's number.

"Please state your name, and we will try to connect your call," the operator said.

"Wynter Lewis," I said.

I waited for the phone to connect and heard Randell's voice.

"Wynter! Wynter, they ain't raping you, are they?" he said, crying. I couldn't help but chuckle because I swear Randell was dramatic.

"Randell, I am in the county jail, not prison," I said, chuckling.

"I knowwww but what happened Wynter baby," he said sounding so sincere.

"I can't tell you over the phone. But my bail hearing is tomorrow at 9:00 am. Please come. I love you so much, Randell."

"I love you so much, Wynter. I know this shit seems fucked up, and I know it is. But I riding with you. I will be at every court date. I'm gone put some money on your shit too," He said,

"Thank you, bestie. I love you so much. I got to go." I said, getting teary-eyed.

"Wynter, stay strong, baby," he said,

"I will love you," I said.

"I love you too," he said, then hung up. The officer walked me to my cell and let me in. There was a TV, bunk bed, toilet and table. I got on the bed, under the cover, and slept.

"It can't get no worse than this shit," I thought as I drifted off to sleep.

The following week, I went to court and was sentenced to 3 years for felonious assault. I broke down in court as they took me away. Hearing my mother's cry did something to my soul. It crushed me.

5

It wasn't easy settling into the prison life. I silently cried most nights, not understanding how I let myself get here in the first place. It wasn't as dirty as I thought, but it was dirty enough for me not to ever want to come back. I never really ate the food because my parents kept my commissary full, and I always had money on the phone. True enough, I didn't really want to talk to anyone. I was disappointed in myself for how I let myself get in here.

I stayed to myself most days in prison. Most of the girls were cool, but there were also a lot of gangs. That wasn't something I was into, so when this girl named Brownie approached me asking me to join her crew, I politely declined.

I was sitting on the picnic table enjoying some sun when Brownie and a few girls approached me.

"What's up, you Wynter, right?"

"Yeah," I said, looking at her with a raised brow. I first learned to always be alert and expect the unexpected.

"I have been peeping how you move; you will be lowkey. I think you would be a great asset to our crew,"

"Thank you, but I'm good, love, I don't get down,

"Nobody denies Brownie," a curvy black girl said\

"Chill T-Bone," Brownie said, then turned to me.

"So, like I was saying, I want you in my crew,"

"I'm good, Brownie. I'm just trying to make up my time and go home; that's it. That ain't something I'm into, but thank you for the consideration," I said.

Brownie and her crew looked at me and then walked away. I didn't think much of it, but later on, I would find out why I should've just beat her ass.

When the outside rec ended, I walked over to the phone to call Randell. I haven't talked to my bestie since I arrived, and I know he was pissed. Luckily, no one was at the wall, so I could have privacy. I dialed Randell's number and waited for the operator.

"Wynter," I said before hearing it ring.

“Bitchhhh, I missed you so much, hoe. Why are you just now calling me?” Randell said answering.

“I miss you too bitch I swear. I have just been in hermit mode, staying to myself. I have been so depressed, Dell,” I said, holding back tears.

“Don’t you cry, Wynter; don’t show no weakness in that prison, baby. You are so strong, and honestly, you don’t even deserve this,” he said.

“I know, I know, man I-“

“Get the fuck off the phone; it’s my turn,” Brownie said behind me.

“Hold on, Randell,” I said, turning to Brownie.

“The whole row of phones is open go get on the phone,” I said

“I want that phone,” she said

“Brownie, I don’t want no trouble. I’m just trying to talk on the phone to my people.”

“I ain’t trying to hear none of that shit,”

“Wynter, who the fuck is that?” Randell asked.

“Nobody, Randell, so how have you been?” I said, ignoring Brownie.

“I have been-“ he started, but Brownie clicked the button to hang up. Now I was pissed.

“Bitch you dumb? Like you really weird as fuck,” I yelled, getting in her face.

“Do something about then 'cause I’m a fuck with you until I get tired,” Brownie said.

When I raised my hands, the girls behind Brownie ran over. Now I held my own, but they started jumping the fuck out of me. I grabbed one girl and started whopping her ass as I was getting punched and kicked. I didn’t give a fuck; one of them was getting fucked up. My hair was in a ponytail, so they were able to pull my hair to get me off the girl.

“Get the fuck off me,” I screamed.

The fight didn’t last long because the guards ran over and arrested us. We all were taken to the hole for fighting. They were going to investigate what happened, so we would all be there until the investigation was over. At that point, the parties who started it would remain in the hole for whatever amount of time they told us to serve for the fighting violation. I was so mad tears streamed down my face.

My whole body hurt badly. I had multiple patches on my head. My hair was falling out in clumps from the trauma, and my scalp was on fire. My nose was busted, and my lip was swollen. To make matters worse, my parents were coming to visit me the next week.

The holes were all single cells with matt on the floor, sink, and toilet. They gave you food through the slot in the door. I refused to eat that shit. I sat in the cold, dark cell, sitting up against the wall. Roaches scattered around my tray, trying to get their next meal. I laid down, took the thin sheet, and covered my head.

"This shit can't be life," I thought as I cried myself to sleep

****

I stayed in the hole for 3 days, I was so weak from the fight, and it didn't help that I didn't eat or drink anything. They came and got me because after running the cameras they found that I didn't start the fight. They sent me to the nurse before I was taken back into general pop.

After she cleaned me up, she gave me a few IVs because I was dehydrated. I was escorted back to my cell and was relieved to see all my food and things were exactly how I had left them. I walked in and sat on my bunk.

“We made sure no one tried to do anything to your stuff,” I heard. I looked up, and another inmate, Bre, and Officer Samantha were at the door.

“Thank you so much,” I said.

“Your father is waiting on your call,” Sam said

“Yeah, and he made sure that when I go to the store, he gave me money to get you extra since you were in the hole,” Bre said.

“How do y'all know my father?” I asked.

“The less you know, the better, baby,” Sam said, and they walked away.

I decided to make some food and watch TV until it was time for me to shower and call my dad. I knew I couldn’t ask him anything over the phone, so I would wait and just thank him. In the meantime, I thought about how I was going to show Brownie who the fuck she was playing with.

I dozed off and only had time for one phone call when I woke up. I walked out of my cell and went straight to the phones.

"Wynter," I said, and then the operator said it would connect my call.

"Hello?" I said.

"Baby, are you okay?" my mom said crying.

"Yes, Mommy, I am good," I said,

"Hold on, your father needs to talk to you," she said, sniffing.

"Baby, stop crying. She's okay. Wynter?"

"Yes, Daddy,"

"You got my message?"

"Yes, Daddy, thank you,"

"You want that handled?"

"Let me handle it," I said.

"You sure?"

"I'm your daughter. You know what's up with your princess," I said,

"Damn right, I got eyes, I love you. You okay?"

"Yes, I am. I'm good daddy,"

"You won't be there much longer, baby,"

"What do you mean?"

"Daddy had a life before I gave it all up for a pretty young woman who gave me a daughter."

"Okay, Daddy," I said, reading between the lines. My daddy was known in the streets, and that's something he thought I didn't know. My momma would tell me all kinds of stories.

"Alright, Daddy, it's time for lockdown. I love you. Let me tell mommy I love her,"

"I love you too, baby, hold on,"

"Yes, baby," my mom said, crying again,

"Mommy, stop crying. I'm okay, I love you. I got to go lock down,"

"Okay, I love you so much, baby,"

"I love you too. I'm going to call you tomorrow.

"Okay," she sniffed.

"Bae, stop crying. I got her," I heard my dad say before she hung up. I felt so bad my mom was crying like this. She didn't deserve the fear I put on her. I went to my cell and watched TV until I dozed off. I was going to start planning my attack, and I needed Samantha's and Bre's help.

The following day, I got up bright and early and took care of my hygiene. When the doors to our cells unlocked, I searched for Bre. I found her outside on the picnic tables.

“Hey, I have to ask you something,” I said

“I know what it’s about, but your father has already informed us. When and where?” she said, never looking up from her book

“How do you know my dad?”

“Let’s just say my father was a legend, your father is a legend. Legends fuck with each other, and the loyalty is for life.

“Okay,

“You don’t know how you’re gonna do it?” She asked, laughing

“I’m still coming up with the plan,” I admitted.

“Listen during the next rec later; she will be out the hole, and my crew and I will have your back. Sam will be the guard. You got 60 seconds to fuck her up.” She said, walking away.

The second rec was in 3 hours; we had lockdown in 30 minutes. I wasted no time going back to my cell. I got on my bunk and started braiding my hair. By the time I was done, it was an hour before the next rec. I put on some sweats, a tee shirt, and my sneakers. I packed up all my food and shit just in case I was going to have to go to the hole

“Stay ready,” I heard through the door, and when I looked up, it was Sam smiling at me.

“I stay ready, so I don’t have to get ready,” I said, smiling back.

What made it cute was that it was something my father used to tell me.

I finished packing, and they called rec right after

“Alright, Wynter, you got this,” I thought as I walked outside.

When I made it outside, I scanned the lot. My eyes landed on Sam, who nodded at me. I then scanned for Bre, who was at the tree with her crew. I walked over and stood next to her.]

“You ready?”

“Mmhm,” I said. About 5 minutes later, Brownie and her crew walked out to the yard, and I don’t know if this bitch was a dog, but her eyes landed right on me. She smiled and nodded her head.

"Ayo Brownie," I yelled. Her smile disappeared as they walked over to me.

"What?" she said.

"I want some work. You had your hoes jump me, and it's up now,"

"Bre, she with you?" she asked.

"Yep, and ain't no jumping or we gone have beef, and you know how it is with me, Brownie, nobody leaves alive with my beef. I respect you, but how you did her, she wants some work, and I respect it," she said

"Fair enough," She said. They formed a circle, and Brownie and I squared it up

"Now Bre, if I beat her ass, I don't want to hear shit,"

"Brownie, that's between yall ain't no jumping, or it's up," She said calmly.

Before Brownie could say a word, I popped her ass right in the mouth. It was on after that. We fought head up, no hair pulling. Brownie had some go in her, and if I wasn't so mad, she may have got the best of me. A two-piece combo I gave her made her stumble, and that's when I was all over her ass. Once we fell, I slid on top and started punching her in the face.

"Enough Wynter! She is bleeding badly," I heard Sam say.

I stopped and looked down. I felt bad because I had blacked out on her. She had two black eyes, a busted nose, and a leaking mouth

"Let's go, Wynter," Sam said. She gently placed me in handcuffs and took me to the hole.

"That's wtf I'm talking about." She whispered, and I smiled. I sat in the hole for a week. This time, I used the time to journal and really understand myself. I stopped blaming Kelvin and really took accountability. Sam gave me food so I wasn't starving, and I drank water. I heard that Brownie went to the nurse, but she was cool, just bruised up.

Bre got word to me that the beef was dead and that I was respected. After the fight, shit was smooth. I accepted my sentence and even got close to Bre. I found out that she had 7 years left on a 15-year sentence. She killed the man who murdered her father. I also found out that my father is the reason she only got 15 years and the reason she is straight in prison. Her father and mine were best friends growing up. After serving 1 year, I was released on good behavior. From what I heard, my father pulled some strings, and I was free. That man was a mystery, but I loved every minute of it. When I walked out the prison, I walked out a new woman. I had grown so much, and all I had was time to think about what I had done. I vow to never let a man take me that far. I vowed never to lose myself in anyone, and most importantly, I learned to love myself and realize my self-worth.

Summer's Story

1

"Baby, I'm almost ready." Summer yelled as she was getting ready for her boyfriend Peter's show

"Hurry up baby, I have to make sound check," he yelled.

Summer looked at herself in the mirror. She knew she looked good. Summer was a bad bitch; she was 5'5, light-skinned with light brown freckles that graced her face. She had perfect C-cup breasts and a cute ass to match. Tonight was her man's show, and she had to look her best because there were groupies left and right

She wore a half-biker jacket with some leather shorts that hugged her just right and thigh-high Louboutin boots to match. The jacket was red, white, and black and covered her boobs. That way, she didn't need a bra. She left it open for an added sex appeal. After spraying on her favorite perfume, she fingered through her jet-black curls, placed her Cartier frames on her face, and knew she was ready.

“Damn baby,” Peter said as she walked into the living room

“You like?” she said, spinning around.

“I love it,” he said, pulling her into a kiss. They kissed for what seemed like 5 minutes before she pulled away

“Bae, keep kissing me like that, and we gonna be late,” she said

“Shit, you look so good I may say fuck this show,” he said, rubbing her ass.

“Just let me know what we doing cause this shit can come off,”

“Naw, I got Lance and Josh waiting for me,” he said, giving her one last kiss and grabbing his keys. They exited the door and entered the black truck waiting for them.

Summer watched her man as they drove to the venue, reminiscing on how they met. Peter was one of the hottest rappers in the city. She decided to go to his show one day, not knowing she would meet her forever love.

That night, she watched him perform, and she was in the front row, ironically. When he started rapping his love song, he locked eyes with Summer and brought her on stage. He rapped to her while holding her hand and hugged her when the song was over. She walked off the stage but was stopped by his homebody, Josh.

Josh told her that Peter wanted her number and to hang out after the show. Now how Josh knew that was beyond her, but she wasn't passing up his fine ass at all. She did as she was told. After the show, they hung out all night, and they have been attached to the hip ever since.

Of course, Peter didn't know he would fall so hard for Summer either. But it was her beautiful smile and kind heart that won him over. She wasn't a groupie; she loved Peter and didn't treat him like P Money. That was rare. By month 2, Peter and Summer were saying I love you, and by month 6, she moved into his condo downtown with him. That was over 2 years ago, and they were still going strong. Although it seemed like they had the perfect relationship, her father hated the fact that she was with a rapper.

Summer didn't come from a poor family. In fact, her father was quite wealthy. He owned several businesses and felt his baby girl could do better than a rapper. He felt like that lifestyle wasn’t up to his standards. Nevertheless, Summer loved Peter, and there wasn’t anything anyone could say to make her stop.

They pulled up to the club, and the security guard opened Peter's door.

“Aye, two of yall niggas stay with her at all times,” he instructed.

Summer smiled because her safety was always his top priority. Peter grabbed her hand as 3-armed security walked in front of them and 4 in the back.

“We got muthafucking P Money in the building!” the DJ yelled over the mic. Before making an entrance, they walked through the back of the club and into an office. The man handed Peter a duffle bag for his back-end payment, and Peter gave it to his manager for counting. Once the money was secured, they made their way to the main part of the club

As soon as P Money entered, everyone yelled his name. He stopped a few times to take pictures and shake hands, but he never let go of Summer’s hand. Some people even yelled Summer’s name. She gained a big following on Instagram thanks to the man who posted her. They made their way to the section near the stage

“Bae, I gotta go perform and get whatever you want. Don’t leave this section without them two on you,” he instructed before giving her a kiss.

Peter walked off, and Summer got comfortable and grabbed the 1942 bottle out of the bucket. She poured herself a mixed drink and sat pretty. When Peter got on the stage, he had the entire club hype as hell. Girls ran over just to throw panties and bras at him. Summer just shook her head and smiled. She loved that her man was loved.

After his performance, he took more fan pictures, and they got into the truck with security and headed home. Summer’s feet were killing her, and she was glad this was only a 3-hour booking. All she wanted was a hot bath and to cuddle with her man. However, Peter had other plans.

2

They pulled up 20 minutes later, and the driver parked in front of their condo.

"Babe, do you want to take a shower together?" Summer asked

"I wish I could, baby, but I need to get to the studio," he said, kissing her hand.

"Again? I thought you said after the album was done, you were going to be home more," Summer whined\

"Listen, baby, our lifestyle costs money; I have to remain relevant to continue to provide for us. That means getting in the studio and making hits.

"Okay, I understand," she pouted.

"Don't pout; I won't be too long, beautiful. I'll make sure I wake you up real good when I come home,"

"Ohhh, you promise, Daddy?"

"Yes, I promise now. Give me a kiss," he said, leaning in.

Summer stuck her tongue out as Peter sucked on it before they locked lips. They loved nasty shit. The longer they kissed, the hornier Summer became. As Peter caressed her body, she started moving her body to his rhythm.

"Aye, step out for a minute, gang," Peter told the driver as they finally came up for air. When the driver got out of the truck, Peter unbuttoned Summer's shorts.

"Come here," he said, locking lips with her as he slid her shorts off from under her.

"Bae-" Summer started, but Peter cut her off.

"Lay back," he ordered. She laid back and opened her legs as wide as she could in the back seat, placing one foot on the headrest. Peter leaned down and started sucking on her pussy lips.

"Mmmm, Daddy," Summer squealed.

He then started to slowly flick his tongue across her clit as she lifted her legs higher. Taking her clit into his mouth, he gently sucked on it while licking it at the same time. That was something that drove Sunmer crazy.

"Ohh baeee, keep going," she moaned. Summer's eyes were closed shut tightly. Her mouth formed an O as he gave her the best head ever. Peter started licking faster and faster as Summer's moans grew louder. With every flick of his tongue, she could feel herself about to cum. She grabbed his head and began fucking his face the best she could.

"Ohh, here it comes, baby, oh my God!" she screamed.

"Mmhmm," Peter moaned sexily. Within 30 seconds, Summer was cumming in Peters's mouth.

"Ohhh, I'm cumming, I'm cumming," She screamed as her cum filled Peters's mouth.. just how he liked it. Once Summer's legs stopped shaking, Peter lifted his head from his favorite place. As Summer caught her breath, Peter leaned in and put his tongue in her mouth so she could taste her juices.

"Mmmm," she moaned, sucking on his tongue. After kissing again, Summer put back on her shorts and kissed Peter goodbye. She walked into the house feeling so good and ready to shower. She was exhausted from the orgasm and the club.

Summer dropped her shoes at the door and went straight to their room. She took off her clothes and went to take a shower. After wrapping her hair and putting on some shorts and a tee, she had some energy. She looked at her phone, and it read 1:30 am. She knew Peter would be home by 2:30 am, so she decided to go into the living room, have a drink, and wait for her man.

Summer was good and drunk by the time 2:30 am hit, and she just knew any minute her man would walk through the door. She decided to get naked and wait on the couch.

Shot after shot, another hour passed, and Peter wasn't home. She tried to call, but his phone went to voicemail. Although she was drunk, she knew that she shouldn't trip. Her man was the breadwinner and the reason she had over 100K in her account. She took one last shot and went to bed naked.

"Fuck it, he'll wake me up when he comes home," she thought as she drifted off to sleep.

At around 6:30 am, Summer felt a pair of arms wrapped around her. She smelled Peter's cologne mixed with Tequila. He was naked, which meant he had showered and everything while she slept.

"Bae, you woke," he said in her ear.

“Mmhm,” she moaned, half asleep.

“Come show your man how much you love him,” he said, rolling over on his back.

Summer was still drunk and sleepy, but she didn’t care. She would do anything Peter asked. She sat up slowly and straddled him. She slid her wet pussy on his dick and gave him the ride of his life. One thing she would never do is deny her man any pussy. They fucked until the sun started to rise and fell asleep in each other’s arms after.

3

A few days passed, but Summer couldn't help but feel Peter was becoming distant. He would stay out later, and their sex life was dwindling. Summer brushed it off as him working.

The next morning, when she woke up, she decided to visit her father. Jordan Ramsey was a legend. Not because he was in the streets but because he came from nothing and still beat the odds by becoming a multimillionaire. He owned multiple businesses and gave Summer whatever she asked for. Their relationship became strained once she started dating Peter. Peter wasn't disrespectful. In fact, Jordan had to admit he was always respectful. However, he felt like his baby girl deserved more than dating a rapper. He had come from the hood and shielded Summer from the struggle as much as possible.

The life of a rapper's girlfriend wasn't what his baby girl deserved, and he ensured she knew how he felt.

Summer hadn't seen her dad in a few months, so she dressed and headed to his office. She didn't need to call first because her dad was a workaholic; she knew he was there. She pulled her Audi truck into her parking spot and headed for the door.

"Ms. Ramsey, how are you?" the security guard said.

"I'm doing great, Arnold. My dad in his office?"

"He's in a meeting, but go on up, and I'll tell Sabrina you're coming so she can let you in his office."

"Thank you so much," she said, heading for the elevators. When she got on the elevator, she pressed the 10th floor. When she got off the elevator, she greeted Sabrina, who came around and led her to his office.

"He should be out in about 20 minutes. Should I let him know you're here?"

"No, let it be a surprise," she said, smiling.\

"Gotcha. Have a good day, Ms Ramsey."

"You too, Sabrina."

Summer looked over her father's massive office. She walked to the windows and admired the city view. He had done so well for himself. She was proud. She looked at his desk, which held pictures of her and him.

She smiled and looked over at his book self. Jordan was a sucker for knowledge and always encouraged Summer to read as much as she could. Her was, after all, his heir to his throne. Summer walked over to the couch and sat down. She began scrolling on Instagram, liking pictures, and stopped at the image of her and Peter from the other night. He had posted them and captioned it "The one I'ma marry,"

She smiled, liked, and commented on his photo just as the door opened.

"What do I owe this pleasure?" He said, closing the door.

"Daddy, I missed you," Summer said, hugging him.

"I missed you too," he said, kissing her forehead.

"So, come sit, what's new? Do you need anything?" he asked before sitting at his desk, and she sat in the chair in front of him.

"I don't need anything, Daddy. I just wanted to see you,

"Yeah, you've been distant lately, and I know it has something to do with that boyfriend of yours,"

"Daddy, please,"

"Summer, I just want the best for you, baby,"

"But he is the best. He takes care of me, he loves me, and I know you said you wanted me happy, well I am,"

"Right, but why with a rapper?

"What did he do to you?"

"Nothing,

"Well, what's the issue."

"I just want a different life for you, baby,"

"Why I have a great life,"

"Summer, you are the heir to a multimillion-dollar enterprise, soon to be a billion once I go public. You don't need to be in that lifestyle. I don't think it's safe for you. Rappers are into too much. It's something about him I don't trust. I am telling you, your old man knows best. I want you happy, but he isn't it,"

"If you want me happy, then you want me with Peter's dad. We always have security, he takes care of me, provides, and honestly does everything you told me a man should be doing,

"Summer, my opinion will never change,"

"Because you are s closed-minded."

"Because I see through that shit,"

"Okay, let me go. It's getting heated,"

"No, baby girl, I am sorry; listen, let's go shopping and end this debate. As long as you're happy, I can try to be happy with this. I don't want to lose you,

"Daddy, you won't ever lose me. I promise the minute I stop being happy, I will tell you,"

"Deal, now let me cancel everything, and we can spend the day together."

"Daddy, you don't have to do that. I know you are busy,"

"Nonsense, nothing is more important than you. China can wait," he picked up his phone.

"Sabrina, please cancel all meetings and push them to tomorrow. Let them know it is my sincerest apology. Also, you can go home early. I am leaving for the day with Summer. Of course, you'll be paid for a whole day. Alright, you have a good day. Bye," he said.

"Okay, I am all yours," Jordan said, getting up

"I have my car here,"

"Berto will drive it to that condo, and you will ride with my security and me," he said.

"Okay," Summer agreed. It had been so long since she hung out with her dad.

They left the building and were escorted into his Maybach truck. The driver shut the door, and they were off to go to lunch, so they put a dint in Mr. Ramsey's pocket

While on their way to their 5th store, Summer noticed Peter hadn't texted her all day. She checked his location, and he was on the other side of town. The icon was moving, which meant he was driving. She decided to call him, but lately, he has been doing the same thing, which hasn't been answered.

"What the fuck is this nigga's problem?" she thought.

She wasn't the insecure type and never felt like he would cheat, but she was starting to second-guess that theory. Peter's behavior changed, and it was like it had been overnight. Summer didn't like this at all. She felt in her gut something wasn't right. However, she knew she couldn't show any signs to her dad because he would have a fit. She put on her game face and continued to enjoy her day with her dad. Little did she know her life was about to change in a matter of weeks.

4

Summer was sitting at the kitchen island eating breakfast when Peter walked in. She looked at her Apple watch and saw that it was 9:00 am. Instead of coming in late, the nigga started coming in the next morning.

“What’s up baby?” he said, leaning in to kiss her cheek. Summer moved her face and continued to eat her food.

“What’s your problem now?”

“Why the fuck are coming in the house in the next day?

“Summer, I know you check my lo, you know I’m at the studio,”

“Man, ain’t that much recording in the fucking world.”

“You like the way we live, right? Well, I have to work,”

“Peter, please, your ass is hungover or still fucking drunk. You have been coming in all hours, shit if you even come in. Your ass has been distant, not answering, and you haven't fucked me in weeks. New flash I am rich, my father is rich, I don't need this shit," Summer yelled.

Peter walked over to the fridge and grabbed a bottle of water. He took a sip and placed it on the island while standing on the other side across from Summer.

"Summer, I am working, and I don't know what you want me to say. I know you don't need me, baby, but shit, this the life you deserve."

"It's not about you working. It's about respect; you don't even spend time with me anymore. You act like you're cheating on me,"

"Bae, I ain't cheating on you, I love you, you know that." He said, walking over to her.

"Okay, but damn, how much do I have to take,"

"Damn, Summer shut the fuck up nagging; I fucking said okay," he yelled.

"Don't fucking yell at me," she screamed.

"Okay, babe, I'm sorry; how about we spend tonight together. I'm wrong. Let me make it up," he said, pulling her into a hug.

"Okay, I just miss you, that's all," she whined.

"I know, and I'm sorry, baby. I'll do better, and I'll be ready by 10 pm. It's me and you tonight." he said, kissing her lips.\

"Why don't we stay in, and I cook for you. We can spend time with just us here,"

"Bet we can do that, I'll be here. I love you."

"I love you too; let me show you," Summer said, getting on her knees.

"Bae, I would love for you too, but I am so tired from the studio. I just need to shower and get in bed for a second." He said, helping her off her feet.

"Okay," she said.

"Listen, tonight it's me and you, baby, I promise; just let me sleep," he said, kissing her shoulder.

"Okay, baby," she said,

Peter went to take a shower and sleep while Summer cleaned the kitchen. She caught a glimpse of her appearance in the mirror and realized she hadn't done her self-care.

She texted her hair stylist, nail tech, and wax lady for squeeze-in appointments, promising to pay extra. Then, she called her friend Imani to see if she was busy and wanted to be treated today.

“Hello?”

“Hey bitch, what you doing today?”

“Nothing, girl, just working,”

“Call off,”

“Unt uh girl, my bills due,”

“I’ll pay you for the day, and I want to treat you to a nail and wax date,

“Aww, friend, you don’t have to pay me, I would love that. I have been working way too much,”

“No, I know you’re saving for your house; I’m going to pay you and treat you. I just miss you, I need some girl talk.”

“What’s wrong?”

“Nothing, just be at the nail salon by 2:30. My hair appointment is in 30 minutes, so I’ll meet you after.”

“Okay, bet, I’ll be there. Love you,”

“Love you too bye,”

Summer went upstairs and put on a fitted hoodie, matching leggings, and my Dior slides. By the time she was dressed, Peter was sound asleep. She stared at him for a minute, admiring his beauty before heading out. She just couldn't shake the feeling she had.

Summer's hair appointment went quick simply because she kept her hair short. She did a relaxer, wash, and style. She gave Trina $200 and left the salon to meet Imani. When she arrived, Imani was sitting in the waiting chairs, scrolling on her phone.

"Hey honey," Summer said.

"Hey bitch," Imani said, jumping up and hugging her.

The girls were directed to sit in the pedicure chair and handed a glass of Chardonnay.

"Thank you, Vita," Summer said.

"Ohh, this was so needed, I swear," Imani said, placing her feet in the hot water.

"I know you have been working like crazy,"

"Yes, girl, so how are you?"

"I'm good," Summer said, sipping her wine.

"Naw, you lying,"

"I am not everything is fine,"

"Summer, I know you; something is wrong."

"I don't know, friend. Peter has just been acting weird."

"You think he cheating?"

"Shit, at this point, I don't know,"

"So, you just speculating,"

"I mean, he stays out late or doesn't come in until the morning. He snapped on me today, and we haven't been having sex at all,"

"Well, it sounds like speculating to me. You are dating an artist, Summer,"

"Yes, but damn, sometimes he doesn't even answer the phone. Then he says he's working at the studio because he wants to keep the lifestyle, he provides for me. I don't need his money, though, and he knows this,"

"Summer, I would kill to have a man who wants to provide. Peter is a great man; he ain't cheating, and I know you have his location. If it didn't say studio, you would've been crashed out. Give the nigga a break. He just dropped an album, and so did other rappers. He probably trying to stay relevant. You know how the industry is, out of sight, out of mind. He's also independent. Summer, Peter doesn't have a huge label behind him. Everything he does is from his own pocket and talent. I think you should be more understanding and relaxed. That man loves the ground you walk on. I just saw his post talking about you and who he's gonna marry. You are so lucky. So many women want your spot, don't let this shit break yall. Most importantly, the blogs and hoes can't wait until y'all break up."

Summer got quiet because Imani made so much sense. Maybe she was tripping. Peter had never cheated or had a scandal. He never embarrassed her, shit, she never wanted for shit when it came to him. Even if he did stay out late, he was working. Imani was right; she checked that location, and he was always at the studio.

"You're right, Mani, I am tripping. I don't want to push him away with my nagging. I need to understand his career and support him instead of nagging,"

"Mmmhmm, that's all I'm saying, friend, he loves you bitch relax,"

For the remainder of the appointment, Imani and Summer laughed, and Imani talked about her male problems. Summer quickly realized that she was tripping after hearing Imani's drama. She planned to go home, cook and suck her man dry. After the appointment, Summer felt like a new woman; her hair was laid, her nails done, and her pussy was freshly fell off the bone waxed. She was ready for a night to remember.

When Summer got home, Peter was getting dressed and on his way out.

"Hey baby," she said, walking over to him.

"Hey beautiful, you look so good," he said, kissing her lips.

"Thank you, I'm about to start dinner so you can eat,"

"Bae, I got to run to the studio. I'll be back at 9 pm,"

"Baeee," Summer whined.

"I promise, beautiful,"

"Okay, baby, go handle your business; everything will be ready by 9 pm," I said,

"I can't wait; daddy misses you," he said, pulling her into a hug,

"I miss Daddy too," she said, sticking out her tongue. Peter instantly started sucking on her tongue before slipping him into her mouth.

"Mmmm, we better stop before I don't make it to the studio,"

"Shit, baby, let me get dressed," he said, going into his closet.

Summer smiled and undressed. She was tipsy from the wine and horny from the kiss. Peter dressed quickly and left the house. Summer looked at the clock, and it was 6:30 pm; she decided to use her rose and then take a nap. By the time Summer woke up, it was 8 pm. She jumped out of bed and hurried to the kitchen. She decided she would make steak, shrimp, cheesy potatoes, and broccoli. As she prepared the meal, she kept looking at the clock to ensure she wasn't running late.

She ordered some roses, candles, and wine from DoorDash to make it extra special. When the door dash order arrived, she sat the candles on the island

and pulled the petals off the roses. She placed rose petals around the living room and kitchen and arranged the candles. By that time, it was 9:15 pm. She quickly took the food off the stove to cool and ran upstairs to change. Summer took a quick shower to freshen up. She put on a sexy dress and perfume. By that time, it was 9:45 pm.

"Fuck I'm late," she yelled, running towards the kitchen.

She lit the candles and plated the dinner, and her man would wake through the door at any minute. She sat on one side of the island and waited for Peter. By the time 11:00 pm hit, Summer was furious. She drank the whole bottle of wine and ate most of her food. Peter's cold plate and wine sat on the opposite side, untouched. The candles had started to drip on the counter. Summer grabbed her phone and looked at his location. When she saw the studio, she was annoyed but thought about what Imani had said.

Summer was drunk, and when she was drunk, she ain't give a fuck about crashing out. But she kept her cool. She blew out the candles and went upstairs to change. She decided she was gonna take him his dinner to the studio. That would show her support for his career. She rewarmed the food walked placed it in a go container. Before she left, she drank Peter's glass of wine and headed out.

5

When Summer arrived at the studio, she started to get excited. She just knew Peter would be happy to see her. She walked in and made her way to studio 6. As she got closer, she realized the other studios were empty.

"My man is the only one who is working hard," she thought.

The closer she got to studio 6, the more she heard groans. Summer knew she was drunk, but she wasn't that drunk. When she reached studio 6, she realized they were coming from that room. Her blood started to boil.

"This nigga fucking a bitch," she thought. She placed the food on the ground and opened the door. Summer's heart sped up, her eyes were blurry as tears formed, and she became hot all over. She couldn't believe her eyes. Peter was fucking the shit out of someone from the back. Whoever it was was bent over so far she couldn't see. When she heard a deep groan, her eyes widened, and she pulled out her phone to record. They didn't even hear her creep in.

"You cheating ass bitch!" she screamed. Peter jumped back with his dick swinging, and she almost threw up when she saw his best friend Josh lift up.

"Oh my god!" she screamed.

"You fucking gay as bitch," she screamed.

"Bae, it's not what you think," Peter said.

"Not what I think Bitch you fucking your friend. You nasty gay as nigga, I'm going to ruin your life. I'm posting this everywhere!" she screamed.

"Bae, please just let me talk to you," Peter said.

"Put the fucking phone down," Josh said

"Shut the fuck up bitch ass nigga. You were just taking dick," she yelled.

"Bitch fuck you," he yelled.

"Gay ass, yall see this gay ass nigga," Summer yelled into the camera.

"I'll break that phone bitch. Turn it off," Josh yelled.

"Stop, Josh, don't disrespect her,"

"Fuck this hoe," he yelled.

“Summer, baby, please put the phone down. Let’s talk, just give me the phone,”

“Fuck you, you’re lying nasty ass going viral,” she screamed. Before she could blink, Josh lunged at her, causing her to drop her phone.

“Stop nigga. What the fuck are you on?” Peter yelled, trying to break them up. They all tussled, and then Summer felt a hard slap come across her face.

“Josh, what the fuck?” Peter yelled, pushing him to the other side of the room. Summer pulled out her comb knife and ran towards them. She stabbed Josh on his shoulder, then stabbed him in the neck. He went down instantly.

“Summer, what the fuck did you do?” Peter screamed. In disbelief, she stepped back as Josh squirmed on the floor with the knife in his throat.

“Oh my God,” Summer thought. She knew she was going to jail for life. This nigga was about to die, she thought as sirens could be heard getting closer. Summer sat on the floor and cried; her father was right.

Everything after the incident was a blur for Summer. The ambulance came for Josh, and he wasn't breathing. Summer was no longer crying but staring into space. She had blood on her hands, and when the police tried to speak to her, she just looked off into space. She had gone into shock. The police helped her off the floor and handcuffed her. She looked up at Peter, who had his hands in his hands, crying.

"What the fuck are you crying for, you fag! You lied to me! Why would you do this to me? Huh? Me though Peter? Me?" she screamed, trying to break free from the police. They led a screaming Summer out of the studio and into the squad car.

Summer was booked and charged with attempted murder. She never requested a phone call, and she didn't give a statement. She was broken. The man she loved had cheated on her with a man. Thoughts went through her mind. She didn't know what she did to deserve this kind of pain. She laid on the cold bunk and cried herself to sleep. Summer had to wait until Monday to see a judge, and to her surprise, she had a lawyer come speak with her before the court. She knew her father sent her.

Monday came, and she was held without any bond for her crimes. The judge ordered her back next week to be tried for her crime. Summer lost 15 pounds due to not eating much of anything. She was stressed. Her whole life had changed in a matter of weeks. Summer's court date came, and she spotted her father as soon as she walked in. She broke down immediately.

Tears streamed down his face as he mouthed "fight." Something in her clicked, and she held her head high. The prosecutors recommended 20 years for attempted murder; however, her lawyers argued that she was intoxicated and out of her mind. After obtaining video evidence, they argued that Summer feared for her life. After a week, Summer was given her sentence.

"Young lady, I am going to reduce your charge to felonious assault. You have no priors, and you have your whole life ahead of you. I think what you did was a result of anger. However, that young man could have died. For that, I will sentence you to 10 years. 3 to be served in prison and 7 to be served on probation. You are not to have any contact with the victim, and you are not to drink during the probational period. I will also sentence you to anger management classes and therapy. I truly hope you take this time to reevaluate your life and change." She said.

Summer accepted her plea and made one request for the judge.

“May I please just hug my father before I go?” she said between tears.

“The court will allow it,” she said. The guards crowded her as her father walked over and embraced his baby girl.

“ I love you so much! I got you,” he said.

“I love you too,” Summer cried.

They hugged for what seemed like forever before Summer was escorted into a holding cell to get transferred to the prison, where she would serve her time. Summer arrived at the prison, and reality set in. She was taken to a room where she was stripped naked, searched, and given a set of clothes. She was escorted to her cell, and the doors closed, causing her to jump.

“I’m Dee,” a voice said behind her. She turned around and saw a beautiful Hispanic woman sitting on the top bunk. Her long hair was curled and framed her face.

“How the hell did she curl her hair?” Summer thought

"Summer," she said, placing her things on the lower bunk.

"How long you in for?" Dee asked.

"3 years,"

"I got 9 months left in this shit hole," Dee said. Summer laid down and got comfortable on her bunk.

"So what are you in for?" Dee asked.

"Damn, why?" Summer yelled.

"Bitch I'm just making small talk to get to know you," Dee yelled.

"Well, don't mind your business,"

"Cool," Dee said.

Summer adapted to prison quickly. She didn't really have any issues. She only called Imani and her dad once a week. Both kept her phone and books laced. Summer had been in prison for 3 weeks, and it was finally time for her to fill out her commissary sheet.

"This shit is dumb," she thought. She couldn't figure out what was good or not. She decided to swallow her pride and ask Dee for help.

"Can you help me with this?"

"Didn't you tell me to mind my business?"

"Girl, I was mad, damn, my bad," Summer snapped.

"Look, watch who you talking to, I have no problem with helping, but I ain't put you here, so fix your attitude with me,"

"Ugh, my bad. Can you help me? This shit due in an hour," Summer explained. Dee jumped off her bunk and sat next to Summer.

"Okay, look, get you some food; all the chips are good, basic shit like these noodles, cookies, and hygiene for sure. But don't use that generic stuff, or you will break out."

"Where is the hygiene?"

"It's on the back are you blind?" Dee asked, laughing.

"No, I just ain't know it was back," Summer said, laughing.

"Do you eat meat?"

"Yes,"

"So the beef sticks are good, canned fish, but I wouldn't do the chicken. That shit is nasty. Turkey is okay, but I will stick to the beef and fish."

"Thank you,"

"You're welcome," she said and returned to her bunk.

"Do you want something to help me?"

"Naw, just make sure you load up because we only go twice a month."

"Okay," Summer said.

After she was done, she went to turn her sheet into the commissary guard. As she walked back to her cell, she looked around. Some women were playing cards, some arguing, some sitting alone and on the phone. She couldn't believe this was her reality for 3 years. Fighting back tears, she went into her cell and wiped her eyes.

"You good?" Dee asked, watching the TV.

"Yeah,"

"Shit tough when reality hits, but it will get better,"

"How you know?"

"I was the same way; I did 5 years. After year 1, you will see it goes slow but fast at the same time,"

"Damn, what did you do?"

"Drug charges,"

"You don't look like a drug dealer at all," Summer said, laughing.

"Shit I ain't," Dee laughed.

"So what happened?"

"Now, who's my minding whose business," Dee laughed.

"My bad, but for real, what happened?"

"I was riding with my ex; he was a drug dealer. The cops got behind us, and he told me to put everything in my purse because they wouldn't search me. My dumb ass did, and guess what? I was searched. I told them it wasn't mine, but he also said it wasn't his. So they hauled my ass to jail. The nigga took the stand on me and said it was mine. I had a shitty public defender, so I was given 5 years and 3 on probation when I go home,"

"Oh my God, I'm sorry that's so fucked up,"

"Yeah, I've dealt with it; at first, I was angry and bitter, but that does not get you anywhere. Forgiving him and myself is what made me grow as a woman. I couldn't harbor hate because I was only hurting myself. Accepting accountability and forgiving me were the main parts. Still, I did it, and I'm so happy I did," she added. The room fell silent as Summer thought about what Dee had said.

She had hate in her heart for Peter, and she was mad at herself as well. She felt like Peter was the reason for putting her there. Summer realized it was her own actions. She didn't have to stab Josh; once Peter had him away from her, she could've left, but rage took over. Summer said a silent prayer and then silently spoke to herself, asking for forgiveness for putting herself in prison. The tears finally released, and she wiped them away.

"You gone tell me why you in now?" Dee asked.

"Uhh, yeah, give me a second," Sumemr said, wiping her face.

"Summer, it will get better, babe. I know it's only been 3 weeks, but I will also try to get outside. When I leave the cell, you sit here all day. Come outside with me, meet some of the girls; we have some of the best ladies here," Dee said

“Okay, I will, so I stabbed my boyfriend’s friend.”

“A bitch?”

“Nope, a nigga.”

“Oh, you crazy? Why?”

“You know P Money?”

“Yeah, I know him; we listen to him in here,”

“That’s my ex,”

“No way you Summer so cold, the influencer?”

“Yes, man, I knew you looked familiar, bitch wtf?” Dee said.

“I know, man, but listen, so Peter was fucking Josh, and I ain’t know. When I caught them, we fought, and I stabbed Josh, and I almost killed him,”

“Damn, I’m sorry, but that’s also a blessing,”

“What do you mean?”

“Girl, you could’ve gotten way more than 5; shit, you just had a great lawyer,”

“I did my dad, got me a good one,”

“Shit, that’s crazy,”

"Yep, but I am getting over it,"

"Well, your secret is safe with me," Dee said. They watched movies for the rest of the night and talked about their life. They had similarities. Summer felt like she had found a genuine friend.

The next day, after the commissary was dropped off, Summer and Dee hit the block. They went outside, and Dee introduced her to her friends.

"Summer, this is Tiana, Cherry, and Coco," she said.

"Hey girl, how long you in for?" Coco asked.

"5,"

"Well, we all have 10 years, so we will be here with you," Cherry said

"Damn, for real?"

"Mmhmm, so did Dee give you the run down?" Tiana asked.

"No, what run down?" Summer asked, looking at Dee

"Girl, listen, don't get in no gangs, stay to yourself, and don't take sit from nobody unless you wanna be they bitch," Coco said.

“Oh, I don’t swing that way,” Summer said.

“Neither did we, but we are all together,” Cherry said.

“Who?” Summer asked.

“Me, Coco, and Tiana,” Cherry added.

“Oh, y'all in a poly?”

“No, we are in a closed relationship,” Coco said.

“Listen, you may not swing away, but when the liquor gets in you, that pussy starts throbbing; oh, you’ll let a bitch eat it,” Tiana said.

“Liquor?

“Yeah, we make liquor, $60 a bottle; we got a batch being done tomorrow if you wanna try it,” Tiana said.

“We normally don’t give it free, but we got 4 batches going, so we will give you one,”

“Aww, thank you, wait didn’t you say don’t take shit,”

“Girl, you're pretty, but we're just being nice; we not trying to fuck, at all. But anybody else, no, don’t take it,” Tiana said.

“Okay bet,” Summer said.

For the remainder of the day, they all hung out. Summer didn't even notice how fast the time flew. Coco, Tiana, Cherry, and Dee had cracked her up all day. They became a little group amongst the chaos. As promised, Tiana bought a bottle for Dee and Summer's cell the next day, just before lockdown.

"Alright, all I have to do is enjoy Summer. Tell me how you like it," she said and hurried out to her cell.

"This is a big ass water bottle," Summer said, examining the funny color liquid.

"Listen bitch you drink all that; you went be so drunk you went pass out. Only drink half," Dee said, laughing.

"Shit, grab a cup and drink the other half with me then," Summer added.

"Alright," Dee said, hopping off her bunk and grabbing a cup. Dee sat on the chair across from Summer and held out her cup. Summer filled it up and then took a sip.

"Shit, taste like juice,"

"That's because it's fruit, sugar, water, and some other shit I forgot, but it's good," Dee said.

After Summer's 4th sip, she was good and tipsy. The girls laughed and talked about the life they had before prison.

"So you never had a threesome?" Dee asked

"Nope, I didn't even think about it." Summer said.

"Well, my ex and I had plenty, but I always thought I would end up with him," Dee said. Summer looked at Dee's gorgeous face; she had told Summer she got her body done, and it looked great. Summer didn't feel like she was attracted to women, but Tiana was right; the liquor had her throbbing. She shifted in her seat, thinking about how Peter would give her head

"You okay?" Dee asked. Summer's eyes popped open, and she nodded.

"You drunk as hell, man," Dee said, laughing.

"So tell me, how is it with another woman," Summer asked.

"It's fun; I truly think women give better heads than niggas."

"Aint nobody topping my ex," Summer slurred

"You wanna bet?

"Are you tryna flirt, Dee?"

"I'm asking if you want to bet," Dee asked. Summer looked into her glossy eyes and knew she was serious.

"Fuck it, let me get this nut off," she thought.

"Let's bet then," Summer said.

"Lay back and take off your shorts," Dee said, and Summer did. She laid all the way back, and Dee kneeled before her. She used her hands to spread open Summer's lips before licking the clit.

"Mmm," Summer moaned silently, throwing her head back. Dee's main focus was stimulating Summer's clit, causing a fast orgasm. Within 5 minutes, Summer moved her lips to Dee's mouth. She had a hand full of her curly hair while she gave her the best head.

"Ohhh shit," Summer moaned as Dee licked faster; she could feel her nut rising, but she also felt like she had to pee. The sensation got stronger and stronger. Summer moved her hips faster and faster until she let out a loud moan, followed by squirting.

"Ohhhh shitttttt!" she moaned, trying to push Dee's head away.

"You won, you won," Summer moaned. Dee lifted up and then unbuckled her pants.

"Now, you do the same thing to me; focus on the clit," She said, dropping her pants. Dee had the most perfect body. She switched places with Summer, and Summer did what was done to her. The way Dee was moaning and talking in Spanish, you would've thought Summer was a pro. When Dee came into Summer's mouth, it tasted sweet; the sweet taste turned Summer on, and she was ready for another round.

That whole night Dee and Summer fingered, tribbed, licked, sucked, and pleased every part of their body. Summer didn't know she could come that much. After that night, Dee and Summer's relationship bloomed. They were both so feminine yet balanced each other so well. As time grew, Summer and Dee fell in love with each other. Dee promised to write, visit, and stay faithful to Summer when she went home.

That plan was halted when Summer got called to the meeting room 8 months later. When Summer got to the meeting room, her attorney was present.

"Hey, what did I do?" Summer asked.

“Nothing, tomorrow you will be a free woman, Summer,” she said, sliding over the paperwork.

“What?

“The judge will be releasing you on good behavior; the rest of your time will served on probation. Do not miss a meeting, don’t test dirty, or they will put you back in here,”

“Are you serious?” Summer said, crying.

“Yes, your dad will be here to get you tomorrow,” She said, standing up.

“Thank you so much,”

“Thank your dad, baby,” she said, winking.

Summer walked back to her cell with mixed emotions. She was going home after only 8 months of time. When she got back to her cell, she woke Dee up.

“Babe, get up,”

“Mami, you know I hate being woke up,” Dee groaned.

“I’m going home tomorrow,” Summer said.

“What? How?” Dee said, popping up.

"I don't know; my lawyer said the judge gave me good behavior,"

"That's great, Summer. Why are you looking like that?" Dee asked.

"What about us?"

"Bitch I get out next month, what are you worried about?"

"You in here by yourself,"

"I was alone before you, I'll be fine, and I won't cheat on you either," She said, kissing Summer on the lips.

"Promise?"

"Yes,"

"Okay, take all the food and stuff. I'm going to write to you and make sure the money is on the phone. Listen, call this number tomorrow and ask for me. I will have a phone by then," Summer said, giving her Imani's number.

"Mami, you know I hate being woke up," Dee groaned.

"I'm going home tomorrow," Summer said.

"What? How?" Dee said, popping up.

"I don't know. My lawyer said the judge gave me good behavior,"

"That's great, Summer. Why are you looking like that?" Dee asked.

"What about us?"

"Bitch I get out next month, what are you worried about?"

"You in here by yourself,"

"I was alone before you, I'll be fine, and I won't cheat on you either," She said, kissing Summer.

"Promise?"

"Yes,"

"Okay, take all the food and stuff. I'm going to write to you and make sure the money is on the phone. Listen, call this number tomorrow and ask for me. I will have a phone by then," Summer said, giving her Imani's number.

"Okay, I will now come sit on my face. I'm going to miss you," Dee said. Summer did exactly as she was told. The following day, Summer left everything besides her walking papers.

"Daddy!" she screamed as she ran out the gates.

"My baby, I missed you!" he said, hugging up.

"Hey bitch!" Imani said, getting out of the car.

"Girl, I didn't know you were here! I missed you!" Summer said, hugging her. They all got in the car, and her father gave her two keys.

"This is to your new Audi truck, and this is to your condo. Imani went shopping and got you all the new shit. The house is furnished and stocked up. It's paid for. I also put money in your account and will do so every month automatically. Here is your new cell phone. The number is in your notes," Jordan said, handing her an iPhone.

"Thank you so much, Daddy," Summer said.

"Imani, someone name Dee gone call you, give her my number please,"

"Dee?" they said in unison

"Yes,"

"You a lesbian friend?" Imani asked.

"Kind of,"

"Well, at least it ain't a no-good nigga," Jordan said. They all laughed and took Summer to her new condo.

As promised, Summer did everything she said she would regarding Dee. She bought her clothes since they liked the same things, bags, and shoes for her to come home. Dee was paroled to her mom's house but would live with Summer.

Summer never saw or heard from Peter; she would see him on blogs but never paid attention. She was in love with a woman and finally found her worth. She forgave herself and accepted accountability for her actions.

The End

Made in the USA
Columbia, SC
15 April 2025

56658629R00072